W9-AYL-085
For
Mary
Keith Baker
1992
Thanks for
bringing me to your
school!

The Dove's Letter

Written and illustrated by
KEITH BAKER

Harcourt Brace Jovanovich, Publishers
San Diego New York London

Library of Congress Cataloging-in-Publication Data
Baker, Keith, 1953-
The dove's letter.
Summary: As dove tries to deliver an unaddressed letter she finds to its rightful owner, she brings great pleasure to each person who reads it.
[1. Letters—Fiction. 2. Pigeons—Fiction]
I. Title
PZ7.B17427Do 1988 [E] 87-8530
ISBN 0-15-224133-7

Printed in the United States of America
First edition
A B C D E

HBJ

The illustrations in this book were done in Liquitex acrylics on illustration board.
The text type was set in Raleigh Medium by Thompson Type, San Diego, California.
The display type was hand-lettered by Judythe Sieck.
Printed by Holyoke Lithograph Company, Springfield, Massachusetts
Bound by Horowitz/Rae Book Manufacturers, Inc., Fairfield, New Jersey
Production supervision by Warren Wallerstein and Ginger Boyer
Designed by Judythe Sieck

For my parents

"A perfect day for flying," thought the dove as she opened her wings to catch a breeze. Up she sailed into the blue sky to see what she might see.

Thc air was so clear and the sun so bright that the dove could count the petals on the wildflowers below. But something caught the dove's eye that was not a wildflower, nor was it a leaf or a plant or an animal or a rock or a log. What caught her eye lay so square and silent upon the ground that the dove knew it must be lost or forgotten. She flew down for a closer look.

"Someone has lost a letter," the dove said to herself. There were no markings on the outside—not even a stamp—so the dove untied the ribbon that bound it together. A letter with elegant writing on delicate paper unfolded before her. Though the dove could not read the message, she knew it must be a very special one to be in such a beautiful letter.

"A letter is written to be delivered," thought the dove. "And since this is a very special letter, I must give it a very special delivery."

And away she flew to see who she might see.

Whoosh-chop! Whoosh-chop! The dove heard a woodsman working below.

"Are you the new mail carrier?" the woodsman asked when the dove flew down and gave him the letter. The woodsman untied the ribbon, opened the letter, and began to read. He smiled a smile as wide as the wedge he had cut in the trunk of the tree.

The dove thought that the letter must be his, and her search had ended as quickly as it had begun.

"Though the letter has no name on it, I can tell by the ribbon that my wife made this letter, for she wears a ribbon of this same color, and just this morning she tied it in her hair."

Then the woodsman ran off so excitedly that he forgot his ax and the letter.

"Maybe it's his, and maybe it isn't. A letter this special should not be left behind," thought the dove as she picked up the letter and flew away to see who she might see.

"Carrots, pumpkins, and peas—I've grown every vegetable you please!" sang the farmer as she worked in her garden. The dove flew down to meet her. "My scarecrow doesn't seem to be working," laughed the farmer, and she took the letter from the dove.

As she read, an expression as bright and full as a sunflower blossomed across her face. The dove knew the letter must be hers.

"I can tell by the chips of wood and the smell of the forest that my

husband made this letter, for he is a carpenter and is building furniture from wood just like this."

She held the letter over her heart and squeezed it tightly. "I'd hug him, too, if he were here," she said and ran off so quickly that she left her vegetable basket and the letter behind in the garden.

"Was it hers?" the dove wondered. "A letter this special should not be left behind." And away she flew to see who she might see.

A sweet and savory aroma drifted through the air, and the dove saw a baker delivering a batch of steaming pies.

"The mail is early today," the baker said as he took the letter with his flour-covered hands. As he read, a tear of joy as big as a blueberry rolled down his cheek. The dove was happy for the baker and happy, too, that her search had ended.

"I can tell from this button mark that my daughter made this letter for me because her dress has a button this same size and shape. Now I'll surprise her!" And he grabbed the biggest pie and ran off, leaving the other pies and the letter behind.

"Was it his? A letter this special should not be left behind," said the dove, and away she flew to see who she might see.

Clip, a-clop, clip, a-clop beat the hooves of a white horse as it passed through the village. The dove knew a horse of this color was a lucky sign, so she flew down to meet the rider.

"You don't look like a carrier pigeon," the young girl said, "but I'll gladly take your letter." As she read, her eyes lit up like the noonday sun, and the dove thought the white horse really had brought luck this time.

"I can tell by the flour upon this letter that it was written by my

mother, for today is her baking day. She should be taking hot loaves of bread out of the oven just now. I can almost taste them—giddyup!"

When she turned her horse and galloped away, the dove and the letter were thrown tumbling and spinning high into the air. Though she tried, the dove could not catch the letter before it landed on the muddy road.

"I still have the letter, and a letter this special should not be left behind," she said, and away she flew to see who she might see.

"Over, under, back, and through, I weave to make a gift for you," chanted the weaver, and the dove flew down and landed on her window box.

"Since when does my mail come from the sky?" the weaver asked as she took the letter and began to read. Her cheeks grew red as two balls of crimson yarn. Now, the dove thought, she could finally end her search.

"I can tell by the mud and dirt that this letter was written by my son. He loves to play outside, and he's almost always covered with dirt. Now I'll give him this scarf I've just woven."

Snip, clip, snap, the weaver cut the scarf from the loom and bustled away in such a hurry that she left the letter resting on the loom and the dove resting on the window box.

The letter had grown heavy as her search had grown long, but the dove knew she must continue. After resting awhile, the dove flew away to see who she might see.

The dove heard the spinning and whirling of a potter's wheel as a potter shaped a mound of clay. The potter raised his head as the dove flew down beside him.

"That fluttering sounds like a dove," said the blind potter, and the dove put the letter in his open hands. The potter touched and felt it tenderly; then he smiled a smile as big as one of his ceramic bowls. This time the dove was sure.

"I can tell from this piece of yarn that my son made this letter, for he always wears a sweater knitted from this same wool. I must go ask him what message he has for me." The potter ran off without finishing the bowl and—just as all the others—without taking the letter.

All day long the letter had been left behind. Now the sun had begun to set, and the dove knew she must start her flight home to beat the darkness and the sleep she felt coming on.

"A traveler—no, a soldier—walks below me," the dove said to herself.

"But it is too late, and I am too tired and too sleepy to stop."

"But maybe the letter is his," thought the dove. When she flew down to meet him, her fluttering wings startled the soldier, who was very near sleep himself.

"Be off! Get away! Don't bother me! I am tired and have many more miles to go in the darkness. Why should I be getting a letter? I have been away for so long that I am forgotten by those who know me," he said. But the soldier took the letter and began to read.

Then the soldier dropped to his knees, and the dove thought of how long his journey must have been and how tired he must be.

"No, this letter is not mine. I have been in battle for many years, and I have forgotten about the feeling this letter speaks of, though once I knew it well. This letter reminds me of a time before and gives me hope. Please, let me keep it to deliver to someone whose love I once knew."

But the dove did not hear, for she had fallen asleep on his shoulder.

"You must have been searching a long time," the soldier said.
"I shall take you home."

And the soldier carried the sleeping dove in his arms through the forest and back to her nest.

The dove slept late into the next morning. When she awoke, she found many gifts, though at first she did not know where they came from.

Then she remembered the day before and the woodsman, the farmer, the baker, the horse and rider, the weaver, and the potter. But the dove could not find the letter.

Then she remembered the soldier. It made her happy to think that she had delivered the special letter after all.

The soldier, meanwhile, thought only of the dove

and the letter and the special delivery he was about to make.

So strong and
high and true,
Like a dove,
I wish my love
Could fly to you.